Alexander W. Wayman

The Life of Rev. James Alexander Shorter

One of the Bishops of the African M.E. Church

Alexander W. Wayman

The Life of Rev. James Alexander Shorter
One of the Bishops of the African M.E. Church

ISBN/EAN: 9783744746984

Printed in Europe, USA, Canada, Australia, Japan

Cover: Foto ©Raphael Reischuk / pixelio.de

More available books at **www.hansebooks.com**

THE LIFE OF

Rev. James Alexander Shorter,

ONE OF THE

BISHOPS OF THE AFRICAN M. E. CHURCH,

BY

Alexander W. Wayman.

WITH AN INTRODUCTION BY

Rev. James H. A. Johnson, D. D.

BALTIMORE:
J. LANAHAN, Publisher,
1890.

Affectionately dedicated
to the President and Trustees of
Wilberforce University,
Ohio.

Introduction.

Every man of merit is entitled to a niche in the temple of fame. A true character is worthy of all.the honor that can be bestowed upon it. When it stands forth in all its strength, it is a conspicuous object for exalted admiration.

A man of character is one who sets his eye upon the right, and, regardless of all opposition, keeps on in the "even tenor of his way." He makes progress against adverse influences, and establishes himself by making non-compromising resolutions.

Men of character are "the men of mark"— men of integrity, who "will never listen to

any reason against conscience." They are
wise men : and it is said—"A wise man will be
more anxious to deserve a fair name than to
possess it; and this will teach him so to live
as not to be afraid to die."

Such men are the substantial men of life,
who live not merely within the cycle of a
generation, but along the course of centuries
and through the rounds of ages. They are
examples for the world, and eminent in this
respect, when endowed with strong mental
powers and cultivated according to moral
law. Thus qualified, they constrain the
depraved to follow them and observe a better
method of living. They do something to
show the value of true manhood, and go
through eventful lives which immortalize
their names along the lines of history.

Such men as these are placed on granite
pedestals, and put where they can be seen as

the representatives of virtue. Statesman-
ship, belligerancy, art, science and religion
have all had their prominent individuals to
be held up for the admiration of the world.
They have been chiseled out of marble,
carved out of wood, and molded out of clay,
that their features might be stamped upon
the minds of those who should come after
them. They have been put in various atti-
tudes to be recognized and honored for their
deeds.

In this wise has been perpetuated the
name of a Moses, a Joshua, a Tubal-Cain, a
Solomon and a Paul. None greater, though,
than a Paul, can be found in the person of a
Sumner, a Grant, a Carlo Dolce, or an Edison.
He whose character is built up on the ever-
lasting principles of religion, effects all
classes of society, and towers up over and
above all worldly representatives; just as

the lofty pyramids of Egypt tower above all surrounding objects.

Those men who have formed ideas of moral greatness, and made them conform to every hue reflected in the gospel PRISM, and have come out in the end triumphant over bitter oppositions, are the men who have fixed themselves so that they never will be forgotten by the righteous, and cannot be destroyed by the wicked. Their path "is as the shining light that shineth more and more unto the perfect day." Men of this order come as the outgrowths of the church —the institution that is greater than the world; consequently, they must be greater than the representatives of the world.

Luther in his gown, is greater than a hero in his uniform. Such men represent the power that refines, strengthens and develops the good institutions of society. This is the reason why their deeds are written down and their forms are lifted up to make their names immortal.

The subject of this little volume, so tenderly and attractively written by the author, was one of those very men who have made themselves "Men of Mark," by building up character. His regard for integrity and his contempt for policy, made him a reputation, as a member of the "household of faith," that was extended throughout the length and breadth of his Connection. He who reads this well written little book, and observes its subject standing before him in all the fullness of his stern, unyielding moral character, will concede him to be a model in Christ, worthy, of zealous imitation.

HAGERSTOWN, MD., July 16th, 1890.

CHAPTER I.

Rev. James Alexander Shorter may be very properly classed among the many good and pious ministers who have filled the pulpits of the African M. E. Churches during the present century.

He was born in Washington, D. C., February 14th, 1817. He was therefore, at the time of his death, three score and ten years, four months and twenty-seven days old.

There was something rather peculiar about him in his school-boy days, that caused some of his school-mates to call him "Uncle James," others called him "Old man Shorter."

His father, Charles, and his mother, Elizabeth Shorter, were born free; and therefore, all their children were free. Charles Shorter, the father of James Alexander Shorter, was known in the western part of Washington City as a man that was engaged in the winter season in the oyster business. It was a custom among those who were engaged in that kind of business, when they went out at night to blow a horn, to let the people know that they were coming. Charles Shorter preferred his natural voice; in a calm night he could be heard at some distance crying *Oysters!*

Elizabeth Shorter, the mother of James Alexander Shorter, for many years kept a stand in the old 20th Street Market. She furnished meals to the butchers and others. By the exercise of proper economy, the family accumulated a considerable amount of money, and purchased a fine property on 20th street, where they lived, and raised a large family of children; and there the father and mother, at a good old age, died.

At the old homestead in Washington, D. C., James Alexander Shorter grew up. After receiving a little education in the day and Sunday School, his parents concluded to give him the trade of a barber.

Rev. Walter Proctor, then of Philadelphia, Pa., being an intimate friend of the Shorter family, was considered the proper person to take the charge of young Shorter. He was sent to Philadelphia, and put with one Mr. Burroughs, who was then one of the most popular barbers of the city of Philadelphia. Rev. Walter Proctor looked after him during his *apprenticeship*, and gave it as his opinion that James Alexander Shorter was one of the most moral and upright young men that ever came under his notice.

Finishing his trade in the city of Philadelphia, he took leave of his many friends and started for the far West to seek his fortune

among strangers in a strange land. He went
as far west as Galena, Illinois. While there
he was convicted of sin, and for several days
wept   as   between   the   porch   and   altar.
There was one hymn he used to sing in the
moments of his sadness; it was this:

> "Come humble sinner in whose breast,
>   A thousand thoughts revolve;
> Come with your guilt and sin oppressed,
>   And make this last resolve."

After seeking for some days, he said he
"found peace, which was joy after grief, ease
after pain, and light after darkness." He
then united with the M. E. Church, there
being no A. M. E. Church in Galena at that
time.

His stay in Galena, Illinois, was short.
He returned to Philadelphia to see his old
friend, Rev. Walter Proctor, as well as
other friends; and while in that city, he cast

his lot with that church in which he was destined one day to be one of the honored Bishops.

There lived in Philadelphia at that time a friend of his by the name of John Freeman. He asked to be assigned to the same class with his friend.   His request was granted.

Having complied with the injunction of the great teacher, Matthew 6 chap., 35th verse, "But seek ye first the kingdom of God and his righteousness, and all these things shall be added unto you," he thought it was about time for him to select a companion for life.   There was a young Christain lady in Philadelphia by the name of Miss Julia Ann Steward; to her he offered his hand and heart and she accepted, and they were married.

In 1838, James Alexander Shorter, with his wife Julia Ann, started for Washington, D. C., the home of his youth, as well as the residence of his father, mother, brother and sisters. He and his wife met a warm reception by the entire family.

He united with Israel Church, then under the pastoral charge of Rev. John Cornish. It was not long before he began to show signs of a coming man. He remained in Israel Church until the Union Bethel Church was built; then he removed his membership there, believing that he could be more useful in helping that young and struggling church than to remain at Israel Church.

The late Rev. John Francis Cook was then the steward, and being an excellent scholar, did nearly all the business of the Church. When he resigned and joined the Presbyterian Church, James A. Shorter was made his successor in office; and no young man was more highly appreciated by the entire membership than he.

About this time there were three young
men in the A. M. E Church in Washington,
D. C., that attracted the attention of the
entire membership. One was James A. Shorter, on account of his stern integrity; John
F. Thomas, for his towering eloquence; and
Wm. D. W. Schureman, the young silver
tongued orator. They were not at all dis-
appointed, for all three of them have made
their mark in the world and Church.

CHAPTER II.

In 1846 the Quarterly Conference of the Union Bethel Church, Washington, D. C., recommended James A. Shorter, and the Quarterly Conference of Israel Church recommended John F. Thomas to the Baltimore Conference for admission. They were examined by a committee, the present Bishop Payne being chairman, who reported the examination favorably, and they were admitted; and when the Baltimore Conference adjourned, these two young itinerants were seen mounted on their horses, leaving their homes for the work assigned them in Pennsylvania; for then the Baltimore Conference extended into that State. James A. Shorter was assigned to Lewistown Circuit as the colleague of Rev. Isaac B. Parker; and John F. Thomas, to Lancaster Circuit, as the colleague of Rev. Adam S. Driver.

The Lewistown Circuit was a long one, and during the winter it was very cold, yet young Shorter was always there at the appointed time.

In April, 1847, he attended the Conference in Baltimore City, which met in Bethel Church.   There had been a minister stationed in Bethel Church, by the name of Henry C. Turner, who had been dead but a short time A great many persons thought young Shorter looked very much like him. James A. Shorter was appointed to preach on Sunday in Bethel, and that part of the congregation who believed he looked like the deceased Turner, became affected and bowed their heads. The young preacher thought it was because he was doing so very badly that caused so many heads to hang down; but, when the matter was explained, it was a great relief to him.

In April, 1848, he was ordained a Deacon in the same church that recommended him to the Conference for admission, and was appointed to Penningtonville Circuit, where he labored successfully. He attended the General Conference that met at Philadelphia, Pa., May, 1848.

In April, 1850, he was elected and ordained an Elder, and appointed to the Lancaster Circuit in Pennsylvania. During the time there, he had the misfortune to lose his wife Julia Ann, leaving him with three children, two sons and one daughter.

When the Baltimore Conference met in Baltimore City in 1851, Bishop Quinn, who presided, seeing how very energetic young Shorter was in the business of the Conference, said, "I am pleased to see how he (Shorter) stands up;" and when he came to arrange the appointments for the ministers, he said to his secretary, "Put down James A. Shorter to Israel Church, Washington, D. C., for I think he is the man for that place."

When the news reached Washington that he was appointed to Israel Church, there was some dissatisfaction expressed—not to him as a man and minister, but, as he was raised there, the members feared he would not be able to command the respect that a stranger would.

Mrs. Lethia Tanner, who had been the mother of the A. M. E. Church in Washington, D. C., for many years, learning that there was some opposition to James A. Shorter going to Israel Church, told him of that fact on the Sunday morning when he was on his way to take charge; but being a man of great discretion, he went to the pulpit as though he did not know there was any feeling whatever against him. His text upon that occasion was, "For other foundation can no man lay than that is laid, which is Jesus Christ.—1st Cor., 3d Chapter, 11th verse; and when he was through his sermon the people began to think perhaps he would do, although he was one of their own boys. He preached again at night and that settled the question.

The members and congregation soon began to rally to him. The Church building was greatly improved, gas was brought into it, and every person believed that the old ship was safe with such a man at the helm as James A. Shorter. He spent two years at that old station, and, perhaps they were as successful as any in his ministry. In

November, 1851, he was married in Israel
Church, Washington, to Mrs. Maria Kerr,
who bore him two lovely daughters. The
mother and both daughters preceded him
to the better land.

CHAPTER III

In 1853 he was appointed by Bishop Nazrey to Bethel Church, Baltimore. Entering upon his work with an energy that had characterized him in previous years, the people soon began to appreciate him as a pastor and a Christian gentleman. His church was in debt several thousand dollars, and he went to work resolving to pay it off before his time was up, and having a grand set of officers who seconded all of his efforts, on one Sabbath, he raised fifteen hundred dollars, which removed all the indebtedness, and he had a grand jubilee, at which Bishops Nazrey and Payne were present and preached.

After spending two years very pleasantly at Bethel Church, Baltimore, he was appointed by Bishop Quinn to Ebenezer Church, in the same city; and the same marked success attended his labors there as at Bethel Church.

At the Baltimore Conference of 1857, he asked to be transferred to the Ohio Conference, which was granted. The Conference passed strong resolutions expressing the sadness with which they parted with him, and asking that God would enable him to be as useful in his new field as he had been in the Baltimore Conference.

After the adjournment of the Conference, he spent a few weeks in the cities of Washington and Baltimore, and then took leave of his brethren and many friends, and started for Ohio and settled at Wilberforce University, where he hoped to educate his children; and his hopes were realized.

After entering the Ohio Conference, he soon came to the front, and was regarded as a man who could be trusted with any Charge in the Conference. He filled all of the prominent appointments in that Conference.

When Wilberforce University was bought by Bishop D. A. Payne for the A. M. E. Church, James A. Shorter and his wife were among the first to give the largest amount of money. He went up so fast in the estimation of the members of the Conference he belonged to, that they began to think there was no man who would fill the Episcopal office with more dignity than he.

In 1864, when the General Conference met in Philadelphia, Pa., it was generally thought he would be elected as the second man, as there were two to be elected.

When the time arrived for the balloting to commence, it was still the opinion of many that he would be elected. There were ninety votes cast, and the first successful candidate received eighty-four, and was declared elected. Jas. A. Shorter and J. P. Campbell received the next highest votes, but neither of them received enough to elect.

There was a recess taken for twenty minutes, after which the Conference reassembled and again had the roll called for balloting; after this, when the ballots were counted, J. A. Shorter was shown to have received the same number of votes counted on the first ballot, but not enough to elect him. J. P. Campbell received the necessary vote, and was declared elected.

CHAPTER IV.

No man ever stood up under a defeat more manfully than James A. Shorter did; for it was a position that he said he never sought, and he would do nothing to elect himself; believing, that if the Lord intended him for that place, he would ultimately get there, and his administration would be blessed. But if he was not intended for the place, he might get there, but would not be a success.

A great many men have gone down under a defeat, and entirely retired from the arena of public life, both in Church and State. Politicians have left the party they formerly belonged to, and the Ministers have left the Church.

James A. Shorter went from the General
Conference cheerfully to his work without
expressing a word of dissatisfaction as to
the action of that body. He served out his
term at the Cincinnati Station, and was then
made the agent for Wilberforce University;
and the next year he was appointed to Wylie
Street Church, Pittsburg, Pa.

In May, 1868, the General Conference met
in Washington, D. C., Israel Church being
the place where it assembled, and also the
Church which James A. Shorter had joined
thirty years previous. As soon as the General Conference had decided to elect three
more Bishops, almost every delegate present
said James A. Shorter would be the first one
to be elected, and so he was.

After his ordination, the Bishops met to
lay off their work. He was assigned to the
unorganized work in the South-west, and

organized the Conferences in Kentucky, Tennessee, Mississippi, Arkansas and Texas; where he still lives in the memories and hearts of both ministers and people.

In 1872, the General Conference met in the city of Nashville, Tennessee. At the close of that session the Bishops changed districts, and Bishop Shorter was assigned to the first district, including the Philadelphia, New York and New England Conferences. To this work he went very cheerfully and organized the New Jersey Conference. He was heard to say that the four years spent in the First Episcopal District were the most pleasant of any ever spent by him. The ministers and people felt, when he was leaving, that they were parting with a father and friend.

In 1876, he went to the General Conference at Atlanta, Georgia, full of Christian enthusiasm; and having been appointed by his colleagues to write the quadrennial address, he prepared it with some care, and it was read by him with ease. The contents thereof gave general satisfaction to Bishops and the delegates composing the General Conference.

At the close of the General Conference of 1876, he was assigned to the Fourth Episcopal district, consisting of the Indiana, Illinois, Missouri and Kansas Conferences, in which district he made a grand impression. He was also made chairman of the Missionary Board, and commenced immediate operations, which were attended with marked success as will be seen hereafter.

The Church had been laboring for years to maintain a mission in the Island of Hayti, but had not met with much success until Bishop Shorter took hold of the work, and in a short time, a missionary in the person of

Rev. Charles Wesley Mossell, was all equipped and sent off to that field.

The missionary was so successful in the work there, that several native youths were converted and sent over to America to be educated at Wilberforce University. All of them graduated with honor. Some of them have returned to their native country to preach the gospel, and one is a successful Pastor in one of the Western Conferences.

The Bishops, ministers and members of the entire church appeared to think that Bishop James A. Shorter was peculiarly adapted to manage the missionary affairs, and therefore he was continued the President of the board while he lived.

CHAPTER V.

When the General Conference met at St. Louis, Missouri, in 1880, that being in Bishop Shorter's district, he was chairman of the Committee on Public Worship, and filled that position admirably. After the three new Bishops were elected and ordained, the Episcopal Committee, for the first time in the history of the African Methodist Episcopal Church, claimed the right to assign the Bishops to their respective districts. The propriety of such a course was questioned by Bishop Shorter, as well as by many others composing that General Conference.

The Third Episcopal District, consisting of the Ohio, Indiana, and Pittsburg Conferences was assigned to him. This being the district in which his residence was located, the appointment in that respect was pleasant to him.

When the Bishops assembled to select delegates to attend the Ecumenical Conference, which was to meet in London, Bishops Payne, Shorter, Brown, and Dickerson were chosen; and they acquitted themselves with great credit to themselves, as well as to the Church they represented.

On Bishop Shorter's return home from London, he resumed his work in the Third District; the ministers and people throughout the entire District seconded all of his efforts, and the four years spent there by him were very pleasant.

Wilberforce University being situated near his residence, the President, Trustees and Students, always had a hearty welcome to his home; several Students lived in his family while they were attending school, and although some of them have graduated and gone out into the world to educate others, as long as they live they will remember "Pa" and "Ma" Shorter, as he and his wife were called by them.

The four years spent in the Third Episcopal District passed away rapidly, and the time arrived when Bishop Shorter held his last annual Conference in the Third Episcopal District, and made ready to go up to the General Conference for the last time on earth; and as there had occurred nothing to mar the peace of his work, the Conferences had all elected good and strong men to the General Conference.

May, 1884, the General Conference met in the City of Baltimore, and in the old Citidel of African Methodism, (Bethel Church), and when the roll was called by Rev. B. W.

Arnett, Bishop Shorter answered to the roll call for the last time at the General Conference on earth.

In many respects that was a remarkable General Conference; for it had been forty years since a General Conference had met in Baltimore City. The address of welcome was delivered by the Bishop who resides in the City. The Quadrennial Sermon was preached by Bishop Brown, and the address read by Bishop W. F. Dickerson.

The Committee on Episcopacy felt it was their duty to assign the Bishops to their several Districts. Bishop Shorter told them that it was a ursurpation of power on their part to attempt to do such a thing. He thought it was unfair to the older Bishops to give them as much work as the younger and stronger ones. He was however assigned to Georgia and South Carolina, and when the announcement was made he said, that work was too hard for him, advanced as he was in life.

When the General Conference adjourned in the month of May, 1884, he was soon on his way to his work, and found some parts of it very much distracted, yet being a man of extensive experience and stern integrity, he was able to harmonize the contending elements.

In April, 1887, an invitation was extended to him by the Presiding Bishop of the Baltimore Conference, to visit that Conference, which was to sit in his native city, Washington, D. C., assuring him that he was always welcome, having friends among the ministers and laymen. He accepted, and was there when the Conference convened. He was invited by the Presiding Bishop to preach for him the Ordination Sermon on

Sunday Morning. He accepted and preached to a large congregation in the Metropolitan Church; text, "Behold what manner of love the Father hath bestowed upon us that we should be called the sons of God."—1st Epistle of St. John; 3d. Chapter, 1st Verse. The Sermon was delivered with great energy and power. He said in his remarks that perhaps it was the last time the members of the good old Baltimore Conference would hear him preach, and said that when he was dead and gone, he wanted them to say nothing about him but the truth.

That was the last time the members of the Baltimore Conference heard Bishop Shorter preach. After the adjournment of the Conference he bade adieu to his relations and friends, and went to the city of Baltimore, Maryland, and on Sunday, May 8th, 1887, preached his last sermon in Bethel Church

to a large congregation ; text, "For the wages
of sin is death, but the gift of God is eter-
nal life, through Jesus Christ our Lord."
Thirty-two years had passed away since he
was the pastor of Bethel Church, Baltimore,
and therefore almost a new congregation assembled to hear him   Whilst in Baltimore
City he visited what few of the old members he could find, and then went to see the
inmates at the Old Women's Home, and left a
parting blessing with them and started for
Columbia, Pennsylvania.

CHAPTER VI

When the Philadelphia Conference met on Wednesday morning, May 11, 1887, in the city of Columbia, Pa., Bishop James A. Shorter was there assisting Bishop Ward in the business of the Conference.

Sunday, May 15th, the services were held in the large Opera House. Bishop Shorter was appointed to preach at 11 o'clock A. M. He stated that among the many things which occurred when he was the minister in Columbia, Pa., that he could not forget, was the arrest of one brother Baker, who was claimed to be a fugitive slave from Maryland, and dragged off to Philadelphia. There he had a hearing. The claimant proved his property and the fugitive was given up, and would have been sent South had it not have been for the energy of his wife, who raised the money and bought him.

The meeting of Bishop Shorter and his old friend Baker at Columbia, Pa., was a happy one, and it gave them the greatest satisfaction to know that the slave flag no longer waved over the "land of the free and the home of the brave."

His sermon on that Sunday morning will long be remembered by the large congregation there assembled, for it was the last time that they saw his face and heard his voice.

When the Philadelphia Conference adjourned at Columbia, Pa., Bishop Shorter took final leave of Bishop Ward and the members of the Conference, to meet them no more on earth.

He took the train at Columbia and started westward, calling at Harrisburg to see a few friends and acquaintances; then passing along the beautiful Juniata river, he looked out on the towns of Huntingdon and Lewistown, which was a part of the first circuit he ever traveled. Pausing a short time at the city of Altoona ; then reaching the great Allegheny mountains, moving around that "Horse Shoe Curve," with one Iron Horse in front of the car, another in the rear, he reached the apex, and then went on to the Smoky City (Pittsburg), Pa. There he spent a short time visiting a few old friends ; and then started for his home at Wilberforce, Ohio.

The Commencements at Wilberforce University are always occasions of interest. The citizens of the surrounding cities and country, as well as the Trustees and friends, come from far and near to be present and witness the exercises. The house of Bishop Shorter was always open to accommodate the visitors.

CHAPTER VII.

The Commencement of June, 1887, arrived, the Trustee Board met, and on June 15, 1887, fifteen days before he took his exit to the better land, Bishop Shorter handed over one thousand dollars bequeathed to the University by his wife. He then said, "I now wish in addition to this, to give Wilberforce University one thousand dollars myself. I want to give mine while I am living, that I may know that it is placed to the credit of the institution, and that no one coming after me can disturb it." The Trustee Board adjourned, and the exercises of the commencement closed; the students who had graduated received their diplomas and bade adieu to the President and Professors, and started out to impart to others what they had received at Wilberforce University.

There was quietness about that place where, a few days before, all was excitement and bustle. Those tall hickory and ash trees which beautify the University grounds, were bowing their heads before the breezes of a July morning and the birds were singing in the evergreens surrounding Bishop Payne's adjacent cottage, when Bishop James A. Shorter, early on that morning, Friday, July 1st, arose according to his custom. When the hour for prayer arrived, the family was called in. The Christian part of the family generally read and prayed alternately. This being the morning for some other one to pray, to the surprise of all present, the Bishop prayed himself, and his prayer being so much longer than usual, it attracted the attention of some member of the family who remarked that the Bishop's prayer was long this morning. After breakfast he walked out, looking on those beautiful fruit trees and evergreens for the last time. Returning to his house, he was taken ill, and lying down upon the sofa he said, "Jesus saves, Jesus saves me." The pendulum of life began to vibrate slowly, and still more slowly; the death sweat settled upon his brow; his lips quivered, and thus passed away from the African Methodist Episcopal Church's Constellation, a star of the first magnitude.

> "Servant of God, well done;
>   Rest from thy loved employ:
> The battle fought, the victory won,
>   Enter thy Master's joy."

James Alexander Shorter was a man of such rare excellence that human language, however eloquent it may be, or however ready in the pen of the scribe, cannot portray his character in too glowing colors.

One writer has said: "He was a man of sterling integrity; his honesty was as transparent as a sunbeam. He was the uncompromising enemy of all kind of peculation. His moral character was without taint or blur; no stain ever rested on his fair fame."

His life is a model for all young ministers. Frank, truthful, honest and pure, he has left behind him a name that shall live on and never die. He was a success as a Pastor and Bishop. The churches in Baltimore, Washington, Cincinnati, and Pittsburg, as well as many other places, will tell how well he succeeded.

No man ever had more friends among the children of the church. All felt at home in his presence, both old and young. As a Bishop he was a success from beginning to end. We have many good and great men, but we shall be compelled to look for some time before we find another James Alexander Shorter. We could trust him with our Conferences; we could trust him with our finances; we could trust him with our domestic relations, and we could trust him with our reputations.

After three score years and ten, he passed away without being wrenched and broken upon the wheels of pain. Opened his eyes upon eternity chanting "Jesus saves me now."

CHAPTER VIII.

The members and ministers of the African M. E. Church can look back upon her history for the last seventy-three years, and call to mind the many great and good men who have led on this branch of the Christain army, and they will be surprised that there were such men as Allen, Brown, Waters and Quinn among her Bishops, who could inspire their sons to go forward, lifting up fallen humanity.

Among the Elders without an education were such men as David Smith, Samuel Todd, William A. Cornish, N. C. W. Cannon, Richard Robinson, Thomas W. Henry, Levin Lee and William Moore, who accomplished much for the cause in their day and generation.

Local preachers have been also great factors in the A. M. E. Church. No one who is familiar with her history can forget Joseph M. Corr of Philadelphia, Pa., who was Secretary of the Conferences for years; George Hogarth of Brooklyn, N. Y., who succeeded Joseph M. Corr as Secretary of the Conferences and also as General Book Steward; Abram D. Lewis and John Peck of Pittsburg, Pa.; Joseph Cox, Stephen Smith, Walter Proctor, J. J. G. Bias of the city of Philadelphia; and Joshua Gilbert, John Jordan and Charles Dunn of Baltimore, Md. These local preachers did a grand work in their time.

The itinerant and local ministers named above have all passed away one by one. A very few of the ministers now living ever knew that such men ever lived. "The workmen die but the work goes on."

The M. E. Church will for years refer with pleasure to Bishop Simpson as their great pulpit orator, to Bishop Gilbert Haven as the friend of humanity, to Doctors Bangs and Stevens as historians, to Moffit, Durbin, Guard, Sewall, Cookman and others as the wonders of the age.

The M. E. Church South speaks of Bishop Bascome and Pierce as two of their greatest pioneers. The A. M. E. Zion Church delights to speak of Bishops Rush, Galbeath, and Clinton as three of their brighest stars, and so the A. M. E. Church can always refer with pleasure to the Christian reputation of James A. Shorter, one of the Bishops; to M. M. Clark, Edward C. Africanus, H. C. Turner, John Tibbs, W. R. Revels and A. McIntosh as pulpit orators, and to Lewis Woodson, A. R. Green, Robert M. Johnson and Daniel W. Moore as theologians.

The writer of this small book cherishes a hope that the members and friends of the late Bishop James A. Shorter, as well as the Bishops, ministers and members of the A. M. E. Church, will accept all that is said about him, because it is true, and a great deal more could be truthfully said about his work and labors of love.

In conclusion I will say:

"Live till the Lord in glory comes,
And wait his heaven to share;
He now is fitting up your home,
Go on we will meet you there."

www.ingramcontent.com/pod-product-compliance
Lightning Source LLC
Chambersburg PA
CBHW022202020726
47496CB00008B/2839